Simply Science

SEA TRANSPORTATION

Discover Science Through Facts and Fun

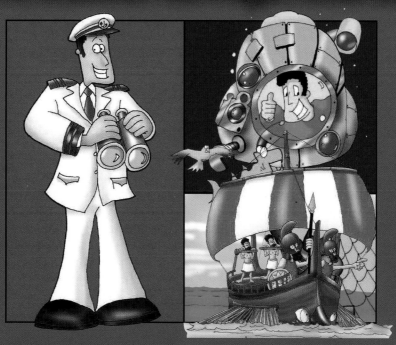

By Gerry Bailey

Science and curriculum consultant:
Debra Voege, M.A., science curriculum resource teacher

Gareth Stevens
Publishing

Please visit our web site at www.garethstevens.com.
For a free catalog describing our list of high-quality books, call 1-800-542-2595
or 1-800-387-3178 (Canada). Our fax: 1-877-542-2596

Library of Congress Cataloging-in-Publication Data

Bailey, Gerry.
      Sea Transportation/by Gerry Bailey.
             p. cm.—(Simply Science)
      Includes bibliographical references and index.
      ISBN-10: 0-8368-9230-5   ISBN-13: 978-0-8368-9230-7 (lib. bdg.)
      1. Ships—Juvenile literature. 2. Boats and boating—Juvenile literature.
      3. Ocean travel—Juvenile literature. 4. Shipping—Juvenile literature. I. Title.
VM150.B252   2008
623.82—dc22   2008012426

This North American edition first published in 2009 by
Gareth Stevens Publishing
A Weekly Reader® Company
1 Reader's Digest Road
Pleasantville, NY 10570-7000 USA

This edition copyright © 2009 by Gareth Stevens, Inc. Original edition copyright © 2007 by Diverta
Publishing Ltd., First published in Great Britain by Diverta Publishing Ltd., London, UK.

Gareth Stevens Senior Managing Editor: Lisa M. Herrington
Gareth Stevens Creative Director: Lisa Donovan
Gareth Stevens Designer: Keith Plechaty
Gareth Stevens Associate Editor: Amanda Hudson
Special thanks to Mark Sachner

Photo Credits: Cover (tc) Scott Pehrson/Shutterstock Inc. (bl) Ricardo Manuel Silva de
Sousa/Shutterstock Inc.; p. 5 P & O Ferries; p. 6 Ricardo Manuel Silva de Sousa/Shutterstock Inc.;
p. 7 (t) Topfoto, (cl) Scott Pehrson/Shutterstock Inc., (cr) Graham Prentice/Shutterstock Inc.;
p. 9 Worldwide Picture Library/Alamy; p. 10-11 Alan Kearney/Photographers Choice/Getty Images;
p. 14 Styve Reineck/Shutterstock Inc.; p. 15 Waterways Picture Library; p. 17 (bl) NASA, (br) Goncalo
Veloso de Figueiredo/Shutterstock Inc.; p. 19 Susan Harris/Shutterstock Inc.; p. 21 SI/Shutterstock
Inc.; p. 25 Bettmann/Corbis; p. 29 (t) Photri/Topfoto, (b) K.L. Kohn/Shutterstock Inc.

Illustrations: Steve Boulter and Xact Studio, Diagrams: Ralph Pitchford

Printed in the United States of America

1 2 3 4 5 6 7 8 9 10 09 08

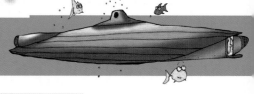

CONTENTS

Traveling on Water

The world is filled with many kinds of waterways. There are seas, of course, and even bigger oceans. Then there are rivers, canals, and lakes. There is plenty of water to explore on our planet...

BUT FIRST YOU NEED A BOAT!

Your boat could be a simple raft

...or a canoe

...or a yacht with big sails

...or a large ferry

...or an even bigger liner.

Pride of Bilbao

People have traveled on water for thousands of years, to explore, to trade, to fish for food, to go to war, or to offer peace.

Even with modern land transportation, more people than ever travel on water. Ships ferry people who are on vacation or going to work.

5

What Are Boats Made Of?

The most important thing about a boat is that it must float. The first boats were logs and rafts. They were made of wood, because wood floats easily on water.

As boat builders learned more about floating and sinking, they started to make bigger ships. They used wooden planks sealed together with **pitch**. The sails were made of skins, cloth, or canvas.

In the 1800s, engineers built ships made of iron. You would think iron would be too heavy to float. But the shape and design of the ship made this possible.

Most modern ships are made from huge sheets of steel **welded** to a steel frame. This forms the **hull**, decks, and main body of the vessel.

Other modern ships are made from a material called fiberglass. Fiberglass is similar to plastic. It is very light and strong.

Sailing ships, built especially for racing, are made from a man-made material called carbon fiber. This material is lighter and much stronger than steel.

The Raft

How can I cross that river?

Early people couldn't swim across wide bodies of water. They needed a boat.

At first they may have floated on logs. Then someone had the idea of tying logs together to build the first rafts.

A Raft to Cross the River

1. These prehistoric hunters have found a herd of deer. But the deer are on the other side of a river, and the river is too wide to swim across.

2. The hunters have to find a way to get to the other side. They might be able to paddle across on logs...

8

Stronger and Safer

The first rafts were likely just logs tied together with strips of animal skin. But later, two logs were added and used as crossbeams. This made the raft more stable.

Reed Boat

In ancient Egypt, boat builders tied reeds together to make rafts. Later, the rafts were curved at the front and back.

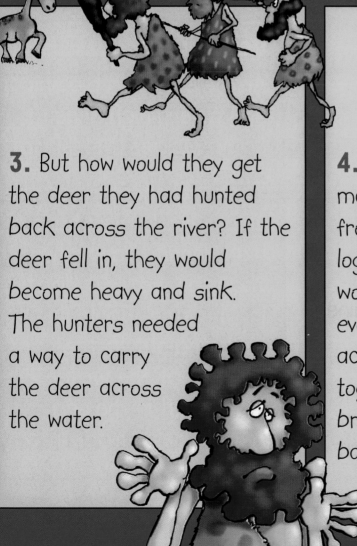

3. But how would they get the deer they had hunted back across the river? If the deer fell in, they would become heavy and sink. The hunters needed a way to carry the deer across the water.

4. The best way was to make a floating platform from wooden logs. This would carry everyone across the river together and bring them back.

Floating and Sinking

When you put any object into water, it will either float or sink. Try testing a few different objects from around the house.

Fill a bowl with water and see if you can float these:

A SPOON?

A BOTTLE CAP?

A PENCIL?

AN APPLE?

Does each sink or float?

What happens depends on the object's weight and its size. Weight and size determine an object's density—its weight and mass.

It is density that determines whether something will float or sink.

Density

All the steel in a big ship has a very high density. So how does it still float?

The steel sheets that the ship is made from have a high density, far higher than the water it floats in. The steel would just sink straight to the bottom of the water if it was put in the sea before being made into a ship.

Luckily, a ship isn't just made up of steel. It is filled with air, too. Air is a lot less dense than water, and the steel and air combined are still less dense than water. So the ship floats!

A loaded ship, like the oil tanker shown above, "sits" deeper in the water than an unloaded ship because it has less air within it.

Displacement in the Bath

A heavy ship will float IN the water, not on top of it. We say it displaces, or pushes away, the water until the density of the ship and the water are balanced.

Let's say you filled up a bathtub so it was completely full. Then you lay in it for a few seconds so even your head was covered. The amount of water that spilled onto the floor would be exactly the same as the amount of YOU that took its place—or that you displaced.

The ancient Greek scientist Archimedes discovered the relationship between density and floating while in his bath.

The Rudder

The first sailing ships were powered by the wind. People could go where they wanted to as long as it was in the same direction as the wind was blowing!

If not, it was best to have oars as well as sails. The rowers could turn the boat, too, though a rudder made turning easier.

A rudder is a flat piece of wood or metal that sticks out from the stern (back) of the boat. It can be moved from side to side against the flow of the water to help steer the boat.

rudder

1. Sailing ships were used to carry rich cargoes of spices and food. But the ships were sometimes blown off course in high winds. The cargo rotted before it got to port.

2. Rowers could be used to help keep the ship on course. But the ships were huge and needed oars with iron blades for strength. These were heavy!

Steering With a Rudder

5. Pushing the rudder left or right turned the ship one way or the other. If you added a long handle to the rudder, it could then be steered from the deck. With a rudder, the ship could be steered in most kinds of weather.

3. Also, oars for powering and steering could only be used in calm seas. Rough, stormy waves would snap them into pieces.

4. A special kind of oar, or rudder, could be attached to the back of the ship to help steer the ship, or at least keep it in a straight line.

Along the Canal

During the 1800s, new factories poured out products to be transported to cities and seaports. There were a lot of goods to be moved from place to place. So canals were dug. A canal is a channel that is dug across land. These human-made rivers connect bodies of water so that ships can move between them.

Soon, many countries had their own canal networks to help transport products. Flat-bottomed boats, called barges, moved under steam power or were pulled by horses.

This canal was cut through high rocks so that large ships could find a shortcut to the sea.

Guided by the Stars

1. Hundreds of years ago, sailing ships were so small that they could only carry a certain amount of food for the crew. If a ship was blown off course, the food might run out before the hungry sailors could reach land again.

2. Without the shoreline to guide them, sailors often feared they might be blown far away to strange lands—or that they might just sail around in circles.

3. According to legend, schools of dolphins guided lost ships home. But it was a much better idea to use the night sky to **navigate**.

4. Navigators learned that if they could locate a star's position above the **horizon**, then compare it with its position when they were on land, they could calculate where they were.

5. An instrument called an astrolabe was an invention that helped make the vital calculation. It was a disc marked with a scale of 360 degrees and a movable pointer attached to the center. Navigators would look at stars and measure in degrees how high the stars were above the horizon. By comparing this with a land chart of the same star positions, they could figure out where they were.

The Astrolabe

Early sailors could figure out where they were as long as they could see the shore. But in open water, they were in trouble until the astrolabe was invented. It helped navigators make accurate measurements using points in the night sky.

An astrolabe was an instrument used by navigators to measure how high the Sun, a planet, or a star was above the horizon.

Oceans and Seas

When the first sailors looked out over the ocean, they could see that the horizon was a curved shape. They thought that the waters might go on forever—even to the edge of the world!

They didn't know how large the oceans actually were. But that didn't stop them from using the oceans for trade and transportation.

If we keep near the coast, we can't go wrong.

Mighty Oceans

Oceans cover a lot of space on Earth—71 percent, or nearly three-quarters, of it. There are five main oceans.

Pacific Ocean

Oceans move around the world as currents, as rising tides, and in waves.

Seas are smaller areas of water than oceans. There are many seas across the globe, including the Red Sea and the Yellow Sea. Bays and gulfs are smaller areas of water that lie around the coasts.

Arctic Ocean

Atlantic Ocean

Yellow Sea

Red Sea

Indian Ocean

Pacific Ocean

Southern Ocean

All oceans are made up of salt water. Salt that is found on land and in rocks is washed into the sea by heavy rains and strong waves.

Traveling Under the Sea

Explorers and scientists have always been excited by what lies under the deep oceans. Until the first underwater machines were invented, people could only guess at the wonders below the water.

Diving suit

In a diving suit, I can do almost as well as a fish!

Skilled divers could hold their breath for many minutes while they explored the seabed close to shore. Then they had to come up again. They couldn't breathe for long underwater. They tried to find a way of taking air with them. As a result, the first diving suit was invented.

Early diving suits were heavy and difficult to move in. They had long tubes down which the air flowed from a boat on the surface. Later, the divers wanted something lighter that let them swim freely. The answer was SCUBA, or Self-Contained Underwater Breathing Apparatus. That made it possible for them to carry their own supply of air in a tank fastened onto their backs.

Submersible

Smaller submarines, known as submersibles, were developed for exploration. They had strong shells, or hulls. They traveled far down into water.

Submarine

The first underwater craft were submarines. They were "mini warships" that could stalk enemy ships under the water and then shoot torpedoes at them. Modern nuclear submarines can stay underwater for months.

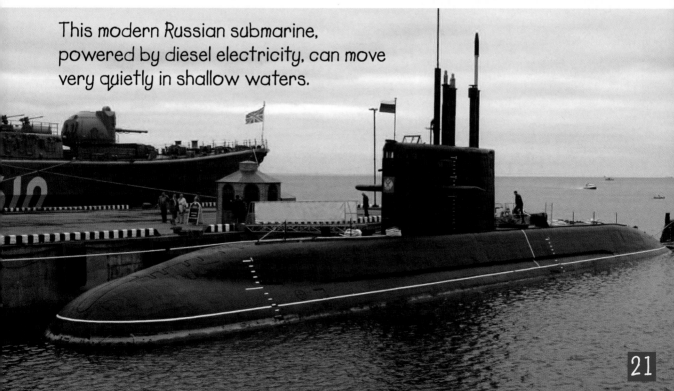

This modern Russian submarine, powered by diesel electricity, can move very quietly in shallow waters.

The Submarine

A submarine is a ship that can travel under the water as well as on top of it. It has tanks inside that fill with water to make it sink. The tanks are emptied when the submarine needs to surface again.

Hiding Underwater

1. In 1602, a Dutch scientist named Cornelius van Drebbel demonstrated an underwater craft. It was actually just a rowboat covered by waterproof animal skins.

2. During the American Revolution, a student named David Bushnell designed a one-man attack submarine called the "Turtle." It hung from the bottom of a boat.

How Do Submarines Work?

To dive:

1. Open the vents and the flood openings.
2. The sub will sink as the **ballast** tanks fill with water.

vents

ballast tanks

flood openings

To surface:

1. Close the vents.
2. Empty the ballast tanks of water by blowing air into them from the air tanks.

air tanks

3. Then another American, Robert Fulton, built a copper-covered sub that could actually sink ships. But it was over 20 feet (6 meters) long—and no one showed much interest in it!

4. In 1889, an Irishman, John Holland, launched a 53-foot (16-meter) sub powered by gasoline and electricity. Its **streamlined** shape helped it move quickly and silently through the water.

5. It took several inventors to come up with the **periscope**. Periscopes use mirrors and are raised to the surface to spy on any ships sailing nearby.

The Bathyscaphe

A bathyscaphe is a craft that can dive deep below the ocean's surface. It is used mostly for exploring the deepest caverns of the ocean bed.

There's so much to explore under the sea.

Up and Down in Deep Waters

1. The craft known as the bathysphere was invented to protect divers from the heavy water pressure at the bottom of the sea. Pressure like this can squeeze the life out of you!

2. The first bathysphere had to be attached to a boat. Divers couldn't explore very far in the vehicle—only what was underneath them. They wanted to go deeper. But the length of the chain needed was too long.

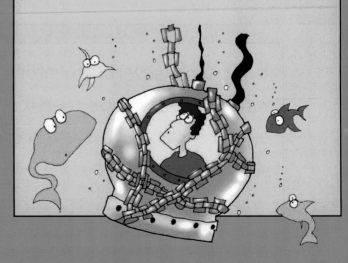

A Two-Part Solution

The modern bathyscaphe is a sphere, or large ball, made of very thick steel. It's attached to a long hull filled with gasoline. The gasoline is more **buoyant** than water and can float.

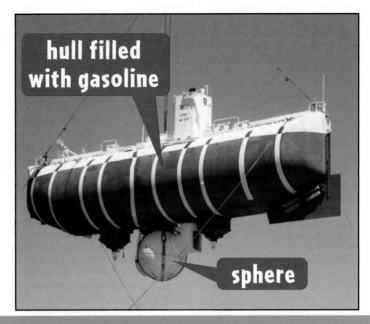

hull filled with gasoline

sphere

3. Swiss inventor Auguste Piccard designed an airtight sphere fitted beneath a boat-shaped hull. It didn't need to be attached to anything.

4. Piccard used gasoline instead of water as ballast, or weight, in the hull. That made the new sphere, now called a bathyscaphe, float. The bathyscaphe could descend more than 6 miles (10 kilometers).

Crawling Along the Bottom

1. Scientists needed a small submarine to explore the seabed. It had to carry three or four divers and be able to stay underwater for days rather than hours.

2. The submersible would need a strong hull to protect the divers. It also needed to carry extra equipment to help divers do different jobs underwater.

3. Small underwater craft that were attached to a ship could dive to around 1,000 feet (305 m). But there were much deeper places on the ocean floor that scientists wanted to explore.

4. In 1977, ocean explorer Robert Ballard and his team used a submersible to find amazing hot water vents, or volcanic holes, on the ocean floor. A whole new world of living things, including strange worms, lived around the vents.

5. With lights, cameras, and lots of action, the submersible continues to help divers map out the seabed and create the **geography** of Earth's oceans.

The Submersible

A submersible is an underwater vessel that can move along the seabed. It's useful for exploring and taking photographs.

A submersible uses its own engines for power so it can move easily along the bottom of the sea. Submersibles often have cameras and floodlights to help the divers see and to light the area so pictures can be taken. Some have mechanical arms that can pick up samples from the seafloor.

Fighting Ships

It didn't take long before armies realized how useful ships could be in helping to win a war. They could be used to transport fighting men. With a large cannon on board, they could also be used to blow other ships out of the water.

Galleon

The galleon was used by the Spanish in the 1500s to transport gold from South America. It was a big ship and not very easy to sail. It had cannons below and above deck.

Trireme

Ancient Greek navies used a ship that had one mast and rows of oars. A ship with three banks of oars was called a trireme. Usually there was a **battering ram** at the front of it.

Aircraft Carrier

An aircraft carrier is one of the largest fighting ships. It has to carry fighter-bombers in its hold and has a short runway on deck where the planes can take off and land.

Hunter-Killer Submarine

Nuclear submarines are designed to hunt down and destroy shipping or enemy submarines. Some carry nuclear warheads.

Battleship

A battleship is a large warship that carries heavy guns. Its guns can be aimed at other ships or at targets on land.

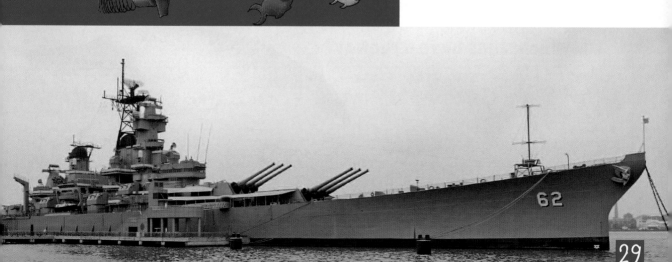

Sea Transportation Quiz

1. Who used a boat made from bundles of reeds tied together?

2. What is the name of the flat blade attached to the stern of a boat that helps steer it?

3. Which animal can help pull a barge?

4. Which instrument helped sailors steer by the stars?

5. How many main oceans are on Earth?

6. What is the short name for self-contained underwater breathing apparatus?

7. What kind of sea craft did Auguste Piccard invent?

8. What product was transported by the galleon in the 1550s?

9. Who used a ship called a trireme?

10. Which ships have a runway?

1. The ancient Egyptians 2. A rudder 3. A horse 4. Astrolabe 5. Five 6. SCUBA 7. The bathyscaphe 8. Gold 9. The Greeks 10. Aircraft carriers

Glossary

ballast: material that adds weight to something; used to cause an underwater craft to become submerged

battering ram: a heavy object used to damage or destroy something by ramming into it

buoyant: able to float

geography: science that studies Earth's surface and its living and nonliving elements, such as plants and animals on the ocean floor, and how they affect one another

hold: the lower portion of the inside of a ship, usually where cargo is stored

horizon: the line where Earth's land and sea seem to meet the sky

hull: the main body, frame, or structure of a ship

navigate: to control the direction or journey of a craft

periscope: an instrument, usually shaped like a tube and containing mirrors and lenses, that allows people to see the surface of the water from inside an underwater craft, such as a submarine

pitch: a kind of tar that is used to make roofs and seal parts of ships to make them waterproof

streamlined: designed with rounded edges in order to move faster

welded: (usually metal) joined together by heating and hammering

Index